The Phantom Hour

Michelle Birbeck

Michelle Birbeck

Dedication

To Mark, for the idea and the chance to play with it.

Acknowledgements

With thanks to Fel for all the editing, and the proofreading. And to the wonderful staff at Argos in Hartlepool for the clock. I promise it's going to a good home now that I've taken pictures of it.

The Phantom Hour

The clock struck one, the single chime loud in the dead of night. Darkness filled almost every corner of the house; the only light seeping in from the streetlights through the cracks of the curtains. The chime echoed slightly until silence took over and washed over the still house.

Mark slid out of bed as the time changed to one minute past the hour. Carefully, so as not to wake his wife, his feet hit the floor and he padded towards the open door. Pausing in the doorway, he glanced back at Kirsty's sleeping form. She looked so peaceful, laid on her back, snoring softly. Her mousey blond hair fanned out across the pillows, almost like a halo.

All lies. Her voice had filled the house only hours earlier, not with the song of an angel, but the screech of a demon.

Mark didn't know what had set her off this time, or any other time, but when she started screaming, it never seemed to end. He hadn't done the washing up right. Hadn't put the plates back in the right order. Had somehow managed to put two grains of sugar too much into her tea. Anything she found even remotely out of sync, she took it out on Mark with her voice and her words.

They hadn't started out so wrong. At one point in their long marriage, the pair had truly loved each other. They'd smiled at each other on their wedding day, excited at the life that lay ahead of them. For years, they'd been happy, missed each other when one was away, talked about how their days had been.

And then everything changed.

It was slow at first. A word here. A fight there. Words turned into arguments, and arguments turned into screaming matches. Kirsty had never lashed out at Mark, not yet. Though in the back of his mind, he realised the time would come when she could scream no more, and her fists would replace the shouting.

He hesitated for only a moment in the doorway, thinking of how it had come to this. Just a moment. Then, he made his way down the stairs in the dark. He didn't want to turn on the light and risk waking her too soon.

He winced when his feet hit the cold tile in the hall, but he pressed on, knowing what he needed to do. Resting his hand on the wall, he used it to guide himself through the night, straight to the kitchen.

Fumbling through a drawer, Mark found the small flash light that they kept there and flipped it on. The beam cut a bright path through the darkness.

There, in the middle of the kitchen island, sitting tall in their wooden block, was the set of knives Mark's uncle had bought for them as a wedding present. Metal gleamed in the light when he pulled one from its home.

Reflected in the blade was his smile—wide and slightly curled to one side. A sense of excited determination played around the edges.

Quickly, he turned the blade away and slid it into the band of his boxers. Nobody had known how his plans had rolled around his mind for months and were now barely hidden beneath the surface of his churning emotions.

Next, he needed the tape. There were neighbours to consider, and screams so late at night would bring them running. Perhaps. Screams were a regular occurrence, so maybe he didn't need to tape her mouth shut. But Mark didn't want to get caught. At least not until he had finished his deed.

Duct tape sitting on his wrist, knife biting into his hip, Mark made his way back up the stairs.

He slipped back into the bedroom and made his way over to the bed. Kirsty was still sleeping. In the dim light, she looked as beautiful as the day they'd married. The harsh lines were gone from her face, sleep easing them into submission. She twitched a little, perhaps from a dream, and turned to her side, facing Mark's half of the bed. In her sleep, she reached for him, her hand searching through the sheets until she could reach no further.

Mark took her hand, threading his fingers through hers, feeling the warmth in them. She sighed, a faint smile lifting the corners of her lips.

It was almost enough to change Mark's mind. These moments when the years of abuse could have been a dream, and when everything became so peaceful and lovely. But he knew that as soon as she woke, there would be a scowl on her face. The lines, deepened with anger, would return, her voice would rise, and all it would take was one tiny mistake on his part, or even hers, to set her off once more.

He reached for her other hand, pulling it over. She came easily, barely twitching at the sound of the tape tearing away from itself. Soon enough, her wrists were bound tight, and her ankles weren't long in following.

Once bound, she started to struggle, as if even in her sleep she knew something was deeply wrong. Her eyes stayed closed for a time, sleep not quite letting her wake up to this nightmare.

As Mark placed the last piece of tape over Kirsty's mouth, she opened her eyes. They grew wide when she saw Mark standing over her, the remnants of the tape still in his hand. She struggled harder when her gaze drifted down and caught sight of the knife handle at his waist.

Mark watched his wife thrashing against the bed, and listened to her muffled begging. He pulled the knife from his waistband, and tapped the blade against her taped lips.

"Shhh. We don't want to disturb the neighbours."

Kirsty ceased struggling, fear bringing out the creases around her eyes. She silenced her pleas, and stared into the face of her husband. He offered her a smile, knowing it was not one she had ever seen on his face before. Not with his cheeks hurting from being stretched wide, and his jaw aching from the clench of his teeth. Leaving the blade against his wife's lips, Mark reached over to the bedside table, and flipped on the lamp. Kirsty winced in the sudden light, flinching away from the brightness. Mark grinned.

"I've had enough," he informed her, leaning in to whisper his words. "I'm sick of the screaming. I'm sick of the fighting. I'm sick of you telling me at every opportunity that I'm not *good* enough for you, and that you could have done *better*."

Slowly, he pulled back, sitting himself on the edge of the bed.

The mattress dipped, forcing Kirsty to roll towards him. Mark ran a gentle hand up her thigh, pausing at her hip, his gaze lingering on his fingers as he caressed her smooth flesh. Memories of another time, a happier time, filled his mind. He'd been so excited when he first saw her naked. It had been new and exciting to greedily devour every inch of the woman he called his own.

Those times were long gone. Now all he saw was the shell in which his life's torment was wrapped. Her skin was still smooth and beautiful, for the most part, but in his mind, it had become cruel and evil.

And that was how he had ended up here, on the edge of the bed at thirteen minutes past one in the morning, brandishing a knife. Plans of blood and death had been forged, thought over and analysed from every angle. Mark couldn't have cared less about being caught. He was consigned to live the rest of his life in a cell somewhere for this crime. All he cared about was ridding the world of this one evil, of this woman who had turned from lover to torturer.

Whether he would call the police himself or get caught by someone missing his wife… he didn't care. But the act itself had penetrated his every thought. When Kirsty raised her voice, he heard that grating pitch and thought of a stab to the throat, one that would turn screeches into gurgles. At the cutting edge of her words, he let his mind drift, imagining slice after slice across her skin.

Bruises and cuts that healed over time did not cover his body, and this knowledge left him torn. The scars he carried were buried deep in his mind. They plagued him when he sat quietly, and tormented him when he tried something new. They were with him always, and though only he could see them, he felt the whole world knew they were there.

"I don't even think you know you're doing it." He started speaking again, tearing his eyes from where his hand rested. "Sometimes I think you don't mean it, the things you say. Then I look at you, and I know. You mean every word. *Every* single word."

Kirsty mumbled something against her tape, shaking her head as much as possible, given the knife and binds. She kept shaking it, until Mark started tapping the knife again.

"No, no. It's too late for apologies. You can't undo what you've done. I need to do this."

Kirsty's eyes went wide again, so wide Mark could see them bulging at their sockets. He raised the knife high, a light laugh escaping him. The look on her face, not the act of stabbing his wife, drew the chuckle from his throat.

Slowly, he brought the knife back down, trailing the tip across her chest and down her stomach. She shuddered under the scraping touch, the violent shiver making the bed shake.

"I could do anything to you now." He met her fearful eyes. "I could kill you so quickly. Just a stab, one quick stab. I could kill you slow, cutting you open a bit at a time until you bleed out. It would take me a while, a long while. But I don't know."

Part of him wanted to take that time. He felt Kirsty deserved the time to be taken over her body, working out his anguish with a knife and her flesh. But he still loved her to some degree. A quick death would be painless for her, as much as a stab through the heart could be painless.

"I know," he said, smiling. "I know what I'll do."

Taking the knife, he flipped it in the air, making Kirsty flinch. "I'm going to start here," he pointed to her feet, "and work my way to your face. I'll leave that for last."

A sadistic pleasure laced Mark's voice as he described his plans to start with her feet, and slice up the soles. Turn her over and work his way up her calves, watching as they split open and blood soaked the bed. Then, he'd turn her back and carve her shins until she screamed, if she hadn't started by then.

After that, once she couldn't run even if she tried, he'd let loose her binds, just to see if she would kick. She might try, he thought, when he started on her knees and thighs, but the kicking wouldn't last long. Soon enough, the pain would take over, and all she would be able to do would be scream.

Her cries would drive his anger, instead of making him shrink away from her in fear. This time, *he* would be the one in control. He would be the one who stood tall and watched the fear grow.

For so long he had fantasised about this night. The last time she'd screamed at him, he'd sat there, shrinking in fear, but there had been a smirk on his face, thinking about his intentions for this night.

She hadn't noticed.

"I think once I'm done with your thighs, I might move onto your stomach." Once again he tapped the tip of the blade lightly on her skin, chuckling to himself when she flinched. "I might carve my name here, or maybe I'll just dig around in all this soft flesh until I find something interesting."

Tears streamed down Kirsty's face now, soaking into the pillow and sheets, darkening her tangled hair. She sniffled, struggling to breathe through her nose. Her eyes were red rimmed and puffy, and a steady whimpering eased out around the tape covering her mouth. The sight made Mark's heart beat faster, drawing his breath in a rhythm that matched his wife's.

But where fear made her struggle, excitement and power made him smile. Finally! After all the nagging, the name-calling, and the threats of physical violence, *he* was the strong one. He had the upper hand, and he used that now to trail the sharp tip of the blade across Kirsty's stomach, causing her to yelp behind her gag.

Mark chuckled. "Remember that time you threatened to gut me?" He glanced down at Kirsty's wide eyes. "No? I do. I remember *every* word you ever said to me. Every threat. Every name. Here's one you might recall." A hop off the bed jostled Kirsty, pulling a louder screech from behind her taped lips.

"We were in the living room. Just after we moved in here. Five years ago? Four? Whatever. We'd just gotten the TV hooked up. Some guy came and had to crawl around the floor for an hour. You… you watched his every move. Eyed him up like a piece of bait on a hook. Then when he left, you laid into me. Why? Because the TV guy hadn't plugged the cable in the right hole! How was that my fault? It wasn't. But still you yelled and screeched. That was the first time."

Mark began pacing the small space in the bedroom between the drawers and the mirror. With each pass he pointed the knife at Kirsty and smiled a sadistic grin. She flinched every time he looked at her.

His wife was suitably scared—Mark had no doubt that she wouldn't raise her voice to him again. At least for the foreseeable future. However, he realised that the foreseeable future might only be a week.

One thing wrong, one slip in her memory of this night, and she would be at it again.

He jumped up onto the mattress, landing feet first, hard enough that Kirsty almost fell off the bed. The strangled cry that escaped her bound mouth delighted Mark.

"You're never going to stop, are you?" he asked, the smile

turning down to a frown.

Kirsty nodded emphatically. She tried to speak around her taped mouth but all that came out were a few strangled syllables.

The noise made Mark lean in close, kneeling down on the bed so he could put his ear to his wife's lips.

"Trying to say something?" He sat back and grinned. "I bet you want me to take off the gag, right?"

Kirsty nodded again.

Though he tried to be stern, Mark's voice came out small as he asked, "Promise you won't scream?"

Again Kirsty nodded her head.

The edge of Mark's knife left a red scratch as he drew it across her chest. Kirsty whimpered.

Without warning, he grabbed the edge of the tape and yanked it free of her mouth. A strangled cry tore its way from Kirsty's throat. It died down to a whimper, and to Mark's relief, she didn't begin screaming for help.

"Be a good girl," he warned, digging the tip of his weapon into the soft flesh of her breast. "If you're not, you know what happens."

"Please," she whispered.

"Please? Please what? Please stop? Please don't hurt you? What about all the times you never stopped? All the times you hurt me?" With a vicious stab, Mark embedded the knife in the bed next to Kirsty. "Why do you hate me so much?"

"I-I don't."

"Yeah, okay."

"Mark...." Kirsty paused, a pained look etched onto her face creating lines where there hadn't been any before. "I love you."

"Bullshit!"

"I do." As Kirsty protested, her voice grew shrill and loud.

"I've always loved you. Always! I just—"

"Just what? Like using me as a punching bag?" Kirsty tried to speak again, but Mark placed his hand on her mouth. He glared at her, staring deep into her eyes. "I want the truth," he told her emphasizing each word. "I want you to look me in the eye and tell me the truth. Did you ever love me? Or was all of this just for convenience?"

He carefully removed his hand from Kirsty's mouth whilst keeping the eye contact. Then, he sat back on his heels and waited.

Kirsty stared at him. There was no malice in her glare, and after a few moments her featured softened into something resembling the woman Mark had married.

"Did you ever love me?" he asked again in a soft and steady voice.

"Yes," Kirsty whispered. "Yes, Mark, I always loved you. And I still do."

The sincerity in Kirsty's voice almost made Mark believe that she was telling the truth, that she had always loved him and didn't mean to do the terrible things she had done.

But a slight tick gave her away. A tugging at the corner of her lips was her tell, and she twitched now, trying to hide it. "Lying bitch!" Mark lunged forward with the knife still in his hands. He didn't mean for it to end up in her chest, but the knife slipped through flesh and between bone.

Kirsty fell back with a pained gasp. She landed on the bed with a thump, the handle of the knife sticking out from her chest like a flag pole claiming some new territory.

Mark stared at the heaving chest of his wife. *It's over*, he thought. All the nagging, all the shouting, was finally going to end. Another part of his mind thought he should call for an ambulance, but as he continued to stare at his wife's panting breaths, he realised that he had murdered her.

Calling an ambulance was out of the question as the realisation set it. Panic galvanised him, pumping his arms and legs, making his heart try to beat its way out of his chest.

"Shit, shit, shit," he muttered, grabbing great chunks of his hair and pulling.

He ran from the room as Kirsty took her last breath. Feet pounding on the stairs, he raced to the downstairs bathroom, as far away from the murder scene as he could get.

For almost an hour, he retched over the toilet, bringing up little more than bile. Once he calmed down enough to think a little clearer, he went to the kitchen and took out a glass. He needed a stiff drink before sorting out the mess.

But one stiff drink led to another, and before long, half the bottle of vodka had disappeared.

Mark passed out on the counter as the clock ticked from 01:59 to 01:00. All the clocks in the house wiped away the hour as though it had never happened.

Mark woke with a pounding head, made worse by the early morning sun streaming in through the kitchen window.

A whistling shrieked through the room, making him bolt upright and look around. Memories came flooding back in a tide of terror and blood.

Shit, he thought. Had he really murdered his wife?

But as he scrubbed his face and glanced around the kitchen, there she was, standing by the cooker. Their old fashioned kettle in her hands, steam whistling out of the top.

"Morning," she said quietly as she pulled the stopper from the kettle. "I thought you could use a coffee. Bad dreams?" She nodded to the half empty vodka bottle.

"Erm… yeah, bad dreams."

Mark's eyes never left his wife as she poured him a coffee and set it in front of him. She then cleared away his glass from the night before and put away the bottle.

When she had finished, she sat opposite him and glanced between him and her hands.

"I think I need to talk to you," she said, finally meeting his eyes for more than a second. "I've been a bitch."

Mark, still struggling to work out what was going on, stayed as quiet as he could. Either the stress of killing another person had broken his mind, or it had all been a dream. On the other hand, this could be the dream.

Kirsty continued, "I've been thinking, and I love you, I do, but I've not exactly been very fair to you. I shout, a lot, and I've wanted to hit you a few times."

Mark resisted the urge to point out that 'a lot' was actually more like on a daily basis.

"And I want to make it better. I want to make us better."

"What were you thinking?" Mark asked slowly, aware that one wrong word might set her off.

"Counselling?"

"For us?"

"And for me."

A frown furrowed Mark's brow. "Not sure what you mean."

Kirsty took a deep breath and leaned on the counter. "I think we need couples counselling, and that maybe I need some sort of, I dunno, anger management?"

Suspicion drew Mark's brow even lower. "What brought this on?"

Kirsty straightened in her chair as though someone had electrocuted her. "I had this… dream, last night. And it made me think. I've been up half the night thinking about it."

"What dream?" Though he was cautious about asking, Mark thought he knew exactly what her dream had been about.

"You killed me," she muttered, hanging her head. "You did it because of how much of a bitch I'd been to you."

"Oh."

"Oh?"

"Not sure what else to say."

"Say you'll let me give this a try?"

Mark nodded, and then said, "Yeah. Yeah, I think we can give this a try."

He didn't mention that he'd had the same dream or that he thought something else was going on. If it all turned out to be some kind of sick joke on her part, then it wouldn't have come as much of a surprise.

Still, it did him no harm to go along with her plans. For the moment.

Six months later.

"Hey, honey, you still all right if I go on this stag night?"

Mark bustled into the bedroom where Kirsty lay in bed dabbing at her nose. She'd been ill for a few days, just a cold, but bad enough to keep her off work and in bed for the weekend.

He leaned down and kissed her cheek. He couldn't imagine that six months before he had imagined murdering her. He'd imagined it so vividly that he'd drunk himself into a state of unconsciousness.

But the next morning, his wife had wandered down the stairs, and everything changed. Their counselling was going well, and her anger management was progressing nicely. Not once in six months had she raised her hand to him, and barely her voice, either. She was a new woman.

"Yes, love, go. It beats you sticking around here watching me sneeze." Kirsty smiled up at Mark, and shooed him out of the room.

This night had been planned for almost a year, but it hadn't been until four months ago that Mark had agreed to going. Once he knew for sure that the reality in front of him was real, he started getting used to the change in his world.

And tonight was the big test, his first night out in what felt like forever. Kirsty trusting him to go out was one thing, but whether that trust would last was another.

The thought of her returning to her old ways crossed Mark's mind only briefly as he met up with his friends. And whatever traces of the nightmare they had shared had long since passed.

Mark felt at ease drinking the night away with his friends, hollering at passing hen nights, that he barely even noticed the time. Hour after hour flew by, until a loud bell announced the closing of the bar.

"I'll get 'em!" Mark cried, lunging sloppily to his feet.

He stumbled over to the bar, pulling his wallet from his back pocket as he went. By the time he got to the bar, he realised that the thing was empty so pulled out his bank card instead.

"You take cards?" he asked the bartender, carefully enunciating each word.

"Purchases over a tenner including food."

"Bag of crisps?"

"Hot food, but throw in some nuts and I'll let it slide."

Mark reached over the bar and clapped the tall man on the shoulder. "Thanks, mate!"

A tray and some careful balancing later, and Mark got the drinks to the table, though each was significantly emptier than when he'd started.

The group downed their drinks in one, and headed out the door into the cold night. On their way to find a taxi to take them home, Mark stopped at a cash machine. The clock on the thing ticked over, as he put his card sloppily into the slot, causing Mark to blink at the machine. Once second it said 01:59 and the next it read 03:00.

For a second, a sinking feeling took root in Mark's gut, but the calls of his friends and the alcohol in his system wiped away the feeling.

Somewhere in the wobbly procession of stags, plans were made for who was sleeping where. Mark offered to take the groom, Sam, home with him as he had the most space and a spare bed. Sure that Kirsty wouldn't mind, the pair piled into a taxi and headed home.

"Just here's fine, mate," Mark said, handing the driver a note.

The pair stumbled out of the car and along the street to Mark's house. Three attempts at getting the key in the lock, and they finally got the door open, shushing each other when it opened too hard and bounced off the wall.

Mark froze, hands on the door, wide eyes staring up the stairs. He let out a sigh of relief at the silence.

"Come on, mate, spare room's this way."

With exaggerated carefulness, Mark shut the front door, and led Sam up the stairs. They gripped the banister with tight fists, putting one foot slowly in front of the other.

"Ssshhh," Mark hissed over his shoulder as they got to the

top. "Kirsty's not well."

"Okay," Sam answered in a loud whisper.

Mark stumbled at the top of the stairs, and caught himself on the banister, making Sam stumble behind him.

As Mark glanced up to check that the door to his bedroom still stood closed, he caught sight of a familiar carnage.

The door was wide open, revealing Kirsty prone on the bed, a knife sticking out of her chest. Mark lunged to his feet and into the bedroom, where he stalled out, hands outstretched as though he could do something about the scene before him.

Sam came stumbling in after him freezing in a similar position. He unfroze first and went for the phone.

The sounds of the call barely reached Mark as he stared out over the dead body of his wife. A knife in her chest, and her wrists and ankles bound by gleaming silver duct tape—something Mark had seen before. He had thought it all a dream, something he came up with in the middle of a dark night.

He sank to his knees in the middle of the bedroom, head in his hands. What he had done that night had disappeared with the hour, but now the hour was back, and so were his deeds. After years of putting up with an abusive wife, he was finally rid of her. Just when she'd started to change. Just when he was starting to fall in love all over again.

Turn the page for an exclusive look at The Stars Are Falling, Michelle Birbeck's first Young Adult Novel, coming in 2014 from The Writers Coffee Shop Publishing House.

The Stars Are Falling

When I came to a stop in front of the dark kitchen window that was acting like a mirror, I smiled back at my reflection. Only for a moment. Then I reached for the light switch by the back door, and clicked it off, saying goodbye to the happy blonde staring back at me.

A night sky replaced the reflected kitchen. It fought the orange city lights as far as it could, until there were too many lights for it to fight against. But up there, high in the sky, the stars shone. Hundreds that I could almost reach out and touch if it weren't for the miles between us. Thousands that I could never hope to count. Millions more than my eyes could see.

One bright star stood out in the night, burning brightly against the Earth's glow. Brighter and brighter, until I thought my eyes must be deceiving me.

I squinted, blindly reaching for the binoculars I left by every window in the house. The old pair found my fingers as if they were searching for me, too. When I brought them up to my eyes,

I panned up from the house at the back of us until I found the burning beacon in the sky.

It filled my vision, wiping out the stars around it.

Dropping my binoculars back down, I looked up at the star.

Only it wasn't a star.

Couldn't be.

Stars didn't fall from the sky. *Meteors* did. There wasn't a shower scheduled, not over this part of the world. One was due somewhere in the southern hemisphere, but even the strays couldn't be seen from back end of beyond United Kingdom.

My telescope was still by the stairs, discarded during the clean-up. I sprinted through to the hall and grabbed it. Back at the kitchen, I wrestled open the bolts, and was more thankful than ever that I insisted a key be left in the door in case of emergency. Not this sort, but it was good enough for me.

With practiced hands, I set up my 'scope, glancing every few seconds at the falling star. Moments later and I was ready to go. Rain wet grass cushioned my knees. It soaked through my jeans, letting me feel the cold of the winter night. Excitement brushed it away, replacing cold with warmth and wet with a persistent need to bounce on the spot.

It took me a few seconds to get the lenses in focus, but when I did…

Whatever type of meteor it was, it was bigger than anything I'd seen before. And closer. Most burned up in the atmosphere, falling to the ground as nothing more than a small lump of rock. This was no small rock.

Fire blazed around the edges, lighting up the sky as it rocketed downwards.

Awe stilled me. I clutched my throat, so overcome with emotion that I didn't know whether to laugh, cry, scream, or dance around the kitchen like a little girl again.

All I managed to do was pan my 'scope along the meteor's path, following its fall.

It ate away into the glow of the night. Where the stars failed, the meteor burned a bright path, ignorant of any lights trying to claim the dark. It was brighter than the moon, the sun, and all the world's lights combined. Darkness gave it strength, making it burn brighter. It blazed a path all the way down.

Until I lost sight of it when it fell behind the taller buildings in town. I sat back on the wet grass just staring up at the night.

Such a beauty to behold!

A shockwave shook the ground beneath me, growling through the dark. My telescope toppled. Glasses fell from the kitchen counter, smashing loudly in the dead of morning. Someone in the house screamed. Lights flashed on in the buildings at the back of ours. But soon enough they plunged into darkness, taking the city with them.

The night sky exploded to life with the absence of light. Stars greedily stole the light from the Earth and gave it back to us with a silvery hint.

As I hugged the ground, quaking in the aftershock, I gazed up in wonder, and one thing caught my eye.

The meteor that I'd witnessed falling may have been the first. But it was far from the last.

Other books by Michelle Birbeck

The Keepers' Chronicles:

The Last Keeper

Last Chance

Exposure (Coming in 2014)

A Glimpse Into Darkness: A Keepers' Chronicles Short Story

Short Horror Stories:

Consequences

Isolation (Free ebook)

Survival Instincts (Free ebook)

Coming Soon:

The Stars Are Falling

Playthings

About the author

Michelle has been reading and writing her whole life. Her earliest memory of books was when she was five and decided to try and teach her fish how to read, by putting her Beatrix Potter books *in* the fish tank with them. Since then her love of books has grown, and now she is writing her own and looking forward to seeing them on her shelves, though they won't be going anywhere near the fish tank.

You can find more information on twitter, facebook, and her website:

Facebook.com/MichelleBirbeck

Twitter: @michellebirbeck

www.michellebirbeck.co.uk